# MOSES
## SEES
## A PLAY

### ISAAC MILLMAN

Frances Foster Books • Farrar, Straus and Giroux • New York

*To my children, Roland and Claude*

Copyright © 2004 by Isaac Millman
Distributed in Canada by Douglas & McIntyre Ltd.
Color separations by Chroma Graphics PTE Ltd.
Printed and bound in the United States of America by Berryville Graphics
Designed by Jennifer Crilly
First edition, 2004
1  3  5  7  9  10  8  6  4  2

Library of Congress Cataloging-in-Publication Data
Millman, Isaac.
    Moses sees a play / Isaac Millman.— 1st ed.
        p.  cm.
    Summary: Moses and his classmates, who are deaf or hard of hearing, attend a play at
their school, and Moses makes a new friend from another class.
    ISBN 0-374-35066-3
    [1. Deaf—Fiction.  2. Schools—Fiction.  3. Theater—Fiction.  4. Friendship—Fiction.]
I. Title.

PZ7.M63954Mu 2004
[E]—dc21
                                                                              2002192881

# AUTHOR'S NOTE

After attending a performance given by the Little Theatre of the Deaf, I decided to have them put on a play in my next book about Moses and his schoolmates. I got the idea for bringing a group of hearing children to Moses' school from a visit to "47" The American Sign Language and English School in New York City. There I watched deaf children communicating with hearing children, using sign language and simple gestures. My continuing gratitude to Dorothy Cohler and Joel Goldfarb, Deaf teachers at the school, for their unflagging interest in these books and for helping me render American Sign Language as clearly as possible in Moses' diagrams, and to all the students and teachers at "47" for inspiring me. And special thanks to Michael Lamitola and Betty Beekman of the National Theatre of the Deaf.

To make the signs, follow carefully the position of the hands and fingers and the direction of the arrows shown in the diagrams. And remember, facial expressions are also important in American Sign Language (ASL).

Moses has devised his own sign for Cinderella to avoid finger-spelling it. Using the sign for the letter "C," he traces several curls.

## HOW TO READ THE ARROWS AND SYMBOLS

➡️ Hand moves in direction of arrow

Right arc

Left arc

↔️ Back and forth

↕️ Up and down

〰️ Wiggle

To avoid finger-spelling CINDERELLA, Moses has devised a sign. Using the letter "C," he traces several curls.

 Several clockwise and counterclockwise half turns

Moses goes to a special school. He and his classmates and Mr. Samuels, their teacher, are deaf or hard of hearing. They communicate in sign language.

Today some actors from the Little Theatre of the Deaf are coming to the school to put on a play. Mr. Samuels has invited a friend, Ms. Morgan, and her class from a school nearby to spend the whole day with his class and see the play. Ms. Morgan and her students are not deaf, but Ms. Morgan knows American Sign Language and has been teaching it to her class.

"Today we're seeing a play," signs Moses.

| WE | HAVE | VISITORS |
|----|------|----------|
|    | fingers touch chest | |

In the morning, the children make posters welcoming the Little Theatre of the Deaf. A boy from Ms. Morgan's class has been watching Moses. He seems to want to tell him something.

THE LITTLE   THEATRE   OF THE DEAF

forward motion

touch chin

Moses smiles. "Hi, I'm Moses. I'm eight," he signs. The boy looks confused.

"Manuel and his family have just arrived in the United States," signs Ms. Morgan. "Manuel doesn't know English or sign language yet. Maybe you two can be friends."

"Moses, you can communicate with Manuel using gestures," adds Mr. Samuels.

I'M

touch chin with index finger

EIGHT YEARS OLD

Moses knows how lonely it can be when no one understands you. Gesturing with his hands, head, and body, he communicates to Manuel that he likes baseball.

"Manuel plays baseball," signs Ms. Morgan.

"*¡Béisbol! Sí,*" says Manuel with a smile.

At noon, the children file into the gym, which is also used as the assembly hall and lunchroom. Moses is hungry. He cups a hand close to his mouth, while Manuel rubs his stomach. They laugh. Communicating with each other will be easy.

WE      EAT      LUNCH

The tables are pushed aside after lunch, and the children get ready for the play. Seated on floor mats, they greet the actors from the Little Theatre of the Deaf by waving and clapping their hands.

The play is *Cinderella*. It will be performed in ASL and spoken English. The actors, Meg, David, Greg, Frank, and Annie, introduce themselves and describe the parts they will play.

forward motion

I     PLAY (ACT)     CINDERELLA

forward motion

1 in passing, touch nose lightly    2

I     PLAY (ACT)     THE MEAN     STEPMOTHER

forward motion

1 in passing, touch nose lightly    2

I     PLAY (ACT)     THE MEAN     STEPSISTER

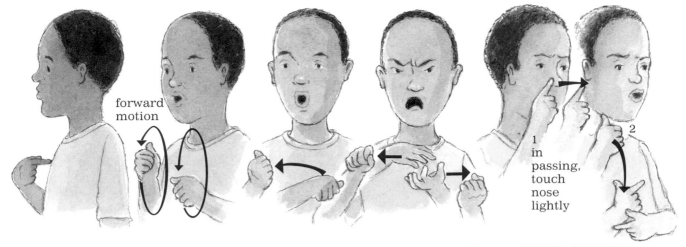

I     PLAY (ACT)     THE OTHER     MEAN     STEPSISTER

I     PLAY (ACT)     THE PRINCE     AND

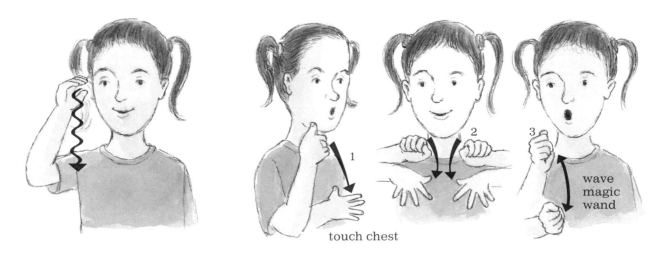

CINDERELLA'S          FAIRY GODMOTHER

The play begins . . . Once upon a time, a girl named Cinderella lived with a cruel stepmother and two mean stepsisters. The stepsisters and their mother are getting ready to go to the royal ball. Cinderella cannot go because she has to stay home and scrub the floor. But Cinderella's Fairy Godmother has other plans for her. She turns Cinderella into a beautiful princess and sends her to the ball in a splendid horse-drawn carriage—with a warning to leave the royal ball by midnight.

Using their bodies, Greg, David, Frank, and Annie create a carriage. Greg is the horse, David the coachman, and Frank is the roof of the carriage. Annie spins an umbrella for the wheels, and Meg, who plays Cinderella, rides inside the carriage.

wiggle index and middle fingers

A HORSE-

DRAWN CARRIAGE

At the ball, Cinderella's stepmother and two stepsisters wonder who the beautiful, mysterious stranger is. When the hour of midnight strikes, Cinderella dashes from the royal palace and in her haste loses her glass slipper. The Prince travels all over the kingdom looking for its owner and declares that he will marry the maiden who can wear it. The two stepsisters try and fail, then watch in jealous rage as Cinderella slips her small foot into the glass slipper.

The King and Queen give a large ball, where Cinderella marries the Prince.

The play is over. The children wave and clap to show how much they liked it. On the way out, they receive autographed photographs of the players to take home.

"I'm hanging mine on the wall in my room," signs Moses.

Mr. Samuels's and Ms. Morgan's students now head back to the classroom. For many, this is the first live play they have ever seen.

I     LIKE     FAIRY     TALES

At their desks, they write letters thanking the Little Theatre of the Deaf for coming to their school. But they are too excited to sit still for long. They want to try some acting on their own.

Moses, Manuel, and Dianne create an elephant. Moses and Manuel are its ears, while Dianne is its trunk.

| ELEPHANTS | ARE HUGE | ANIMALS |
|-----------|----------|---------|
|           |          | rock fingers while touching chest |

Tony, Mary, and John make a camel.
"I'll be a tree," signs Betty.

| CAMELS | LIVE IN | THE DESERT |

"Why don't we put on a play of our own, like *Cinderella*," Mr. Samuels signs to his students. "We'll perform it for Ms. Morgan and her class."

"A wonderful idea," signs Ms. Morgan. "And we'll do one for you. We can start planning for it tomorrow."

"I want to play Cinderella!" signs Betty. She points to Moses and adds, "And I want him to be the Prince."

Mr. Samuels smiles. "Let's wait till tomorrow. Now it's time to get ready to go home."

Before they part, Moses shows Manuel the sign for "friend."

"*¡Somos amigos!*" says Manuel as they shake hands. Then both climb aboard their separate school buses.

I    MADE (MET)    A NEW    FRIEND

At home, Moses tells his mom what happened at school.

I  SAW  A PLAY

forward
motion

AT  SCHOOL.  I  ALSO

clap twice

move hands
over and
repeat

MET  M A N U E L.

HE  HEARS.  WE

COMMUNICATED  USING  GESTURES.

HE'S  MY  SPECIAL  FRIEND.

"Moses, call Grand-père and Grand-mère," signs his mother, "and tell them about your day."

On the keyboard of their TTY, a special Teletype device used by deaf people to communicate over the telephone, Moses types what happened to him at school. His message is changed to electronic code and sent over the telephone line to his grandparents' TTY in France, where it appears on a screen as text.

Moses' grandparents send back this reply:

MOSES,

WE'RE HAPPY THAT YOU SAW A PLAY IN SCHOOL AND WE'RE ESPECIALLY GLAD THAT YOU MADE A NEW FRIEND. ON OUR NEXT VISIT, LET'S PLAN TO SEE THE LITTLE THEATRE OF THE DEAF TOGETHER. WE ARE GETTING A COMPUTER SO THAT WE CAN ALSO COMMUNICATE WITH YOU BY E-MAIL.
WE LOVE YOU.
GRAND-PÈRE AND GRAND-MÈRE